Russ and the Firehouse

Dedication

For Captain Ed Rickert,
Chicago Fire Department (retired)

Woodbine House, Inc., 6510 Bells Mill Rd., Bethesda, MD 20817, 800-843-7323.
http://www.woodbinehouse.com

Library of Congress Cataloging-in-Publication Data

Rickert, Janet Elizabeth.
Russ and the firehouse / by Janet Elizabeth Rickert ; photographs by Pete McGahan.
p. cm.
Summary: Russ, a five-year-old with Down syndrome, visits his uncle's firehouse and gets to help with the daily chores.
ISBN-13: 978-1-890627-17-1
ISBN-10: 1-890627-17-8
1. Fire stations—Juvenile literature. [1. Fire stations. 2. Fire departments. 3. Down syndrome. 4. Mentally handicapped.]
I. McGahan, Pete, ill. II. Title.

TH9148 .R523 2000
628.9'25—dc21 99-058178

Manufactured in China

First edition

10 9 8 7 6 5 4 3

Russ and the Firehouse

Janet Elizabeth Rickert ▪ Photographs by Pete McGahan

Woodbine House ▪ 2000

Once upon a time, not too long ago, there was a little boy named Russ who got a job at a firehouse.

His mom
took him
there to see
his Uncle
Jerry, who is
a fireman.

Uncle Jerry
asked Russ
if he would
like to stay
and help
around the
firehouse.
Russ said,
"Yes!"

Russ got
to meet
everyone . . .

. . . and do all sorts of neat things.

HEY, I have a pretty good aim!
FIRE
CHICAGO
DEPT

Uncle Jerry
told Russ that
a very important
part of being a fireman is cleaning all
the equipment and making sure it works.

Uncle Jerry and Russ
inspected the equipment.

First an ax, . . .

. . . then a fire hydrant, . . .

. . . then a flashlight, . . .

. . . and finally a helmet.

Uncle Jerry asked Russ to help him clean the fire boots.

Boy, these are *heavy*!
HYDRAULIC
DANGER
ELECTROCUTION HAZARD
KEEP CLEAR

Then, Russ helped Uncle Jerry clean the fire ladders.

Russ scrubbed and
rinsed them until they
sparkled in the sun.

This is fun!

Next, Uncle Jerry and Russ gave
Sparky, the firehouse dog, a bath.

When Russ was done,
Sparky shook all the water
off . . . and Russ got wet too!

Then, Uncle Jerry and Russ cleaned the fire truck . . .

. . . and the tires!

Uncle Jerry helped Russ spray
all the soap off with a big fire hose.

But now it was getting late and Russ had done a lot of work, so his mom came to take him home.

The firemen said, “Thank you, Russ,”
and asked if Russ could come back soon.

Russ was excited, and said, “Yes!”
Everybody waved good-bye . . .

And that is
how Russ got
a job at the
firehouse.

The End!

Special Thanks

The Chicago Fire Department

Fire Commissioner:
Raymond E. Orozco

Assistant Fire Commissioner:
Jim Corbet

Firemen of Engine #54
and Truck #20:

Jerry Rickert

Tom Munizz

Pat Delaney

Dan Grosh

Jim Rosner

Lt. Dan Mullaney

Donna Blanke

Luke Mullaney

Beverly Minik

Mark Minik

Mark Rickert

Brian Rosner

Eleanor Telander

Sparky & Dot, ***the Dalmatians***